Mystery in the Night Woods

by
JOHN PETERSON

illustrated by
CYNDY SZEKERES

cover illustration by
JACQUELINE ROGERS

A
LITTLE APPLE
PAPERBACK

SCHOLASTIC INC.
New York Toronto London Auckland Sydney

ISBN 0-590-45224-X

Text copyright © 1969 by John Peterson.
Illustrations copyright © 1969 by Scholastic Inc.
All rights reserved. Published by Scholastic Inc.
APPLE PAPERBACKS is a registered trademark of Scholastic Inc.

12 11 10 9 8 7   0/0

Printed in the U.S.A.   40

To Beatrice and Eva

Bat and Flying Squirrel

THE setting sun made long shadows in the Night Woods. The day animals were going to bed. They were finished with the work of the day. Now the night animals were waking up. It was time for their day to begin.

The rays of the setting sun shone into the bedroom of Mr. and Mrs. Bat.

"Get up, Bat! Get up!" Mrs. Bat gave her husband a push. "Can't you hear that knocking?"

Bat sat up and rubbed his eyes. He heard a loud rapping at the front door. He stretched his wings. Then he swung his feet out of the bed and into his slippers.

"Coming! Coming!" he shouted toward the door.

The knocking grew louder. Bat put on his bathrobe. He pushed a pile of books away from the front door and opened it.

A small flying squirrel with large eyes rushed into the room.

"Oh, it's you, F.S.," said Bat. "Aren't you early?"

"Today's the day, Bat, old friend," said the flying squirrel. "Today's the day you're going to give me a flying lesson."

"Oh please, F.S.," said Bat. "I haven't had my breakfast yet. Look — I'm not even dressed."

"You're always late, Bat," said Flying Squirrel. "If you got up earlier and worked as hard as I do, *you* might be the owner of this apartment tree instead of me."

Bat looked upset. "Please, F.S. — not the pep talk again. It's too early. Now look, as long as you're here, why not have breakfast with my wife and me." He put his wing around Flying Squirrel and led him into the kitchen. "You bachelors don't eat well, I know. You really should get married. Then you would have someone to take care of you. What would you like for breakfast?"

"Just coffee, thank you. I want to get going with the flying lessons. Some day, Bat, I may be able to fly as well as you do."

Bat picked up some dirty dishes from the table. He put them on another pile of dirty dishes in the sink. Then he took some books off a chair. "Here, F.S. — sit here."

"What I want to do more than anything," said Flying Squirrel, "is to fly up to a cloud — and fly right in the middle of it. That must be wonderful."

Bat cracked six eggs carefully and dropped them into the frying pan. "F.S.," he said, "face it. I have wings, and you do not. You will never be able to fly the way I do — no matter how many lessons you take."

Suddenly Flying Squirrel looked sad. He sat down in the chair. "Do you mean that? Do you mean I can never become the best flyer in the Night Woods?"

"I'm afraid not, F.S.," said Bat. "But I wouldn't feel bad about it if I were you. You're a wonderful glider."

Flying Squirrel began walking back and forth. "Gliding isn't good enough. I'm a *flying* squirrel. I want to fly. And when I do something, I want to do it the best," he said.

"Whatever you say, F.S.," said Bat. "If you still want the lessons, that's all right with me. If not — that's all right too."

Flying Squirrel kept on walking back and forth. He was thinking. He stared straight ahead with his large eyes.

"Bat!" It was Mrs. Bat calling from the bedroom.

"Yes dear," said Bat. He put her breakfast on a tray. "Be there in a minute."

Just then Flying Squirrel banged his fist on the table. The dishes rattled. "I have it!" he shouted.

"Whatever it is, will you hold it a minute?" said Bat. "I'll be right back."

He walked toward the bedroom with the tray. Flying Squirrel walked behind him, pulling at his sleeve. "Look at my eyes, Bat. Look at my eyes!"

"I can't look now," said Bat. "I'm trying not to spill coffee." He pushed the bedroom door open with his foot.

Bat's friend paced back and forth outside the bedroom door until Bat came out.

"Look at my eyes, Bat. See how large they are? That probably means I have excellent eyesight."

"Really?" said Bat. "Sometimes large eyes mean you are nearsighted."

"Nonsense!" said Flying Squirrel. "It means I can see better than anybody else in the Night Woods. The bigger the eyes, the better the eyesight. And I'm going to prove it! Come with me." Flying Squirrel pulled at Bat's sleeve.

"Let's have breakfast first," said Bat. "Then you can prove how good your eyesight is."

Beautiful Miss Owl

THREE nights later, Bat and Flying Squirrel were sitting on the top branch of the Sycamore Arms Apartment Tree. It was the tallest tree in the Night Woods. The moon was bright. The two animals could see almost all the way to Bad Creek.

During the day, the Sycamore Arms was a noisy, busy place. It was the favorite lookout of all the tree-climbing animals. There was much good-natured yelling back and forth between the high-climbing animals and the low-flying birds.

At night it was different. The birds were asleep and the treetop was quiet. Now it was moving gently in the breeze. Suddenly Flying Squirrel pointed. "There," he said. "Do you see that? Near the creek? It's Police Chief Skunk."

"How many times do we have to do this to prove that you have the best eyesight in the Night Woods?" said Bat. "This is the third night we've been up here. I'm getting tired."

"Never mind that," said Flying Squirrel. "Fly over there and see if I'm right."

"Oh very well," said Bat. "But let's make this the last time." He flew to the spot near the creek. In a few minutes he was back again. "I'm sorry to tell you that it was not Chief Skunk. It was Miss Owl. That's your first mistake."

"Miss Owl? Who's Miss Owl? I never heard of Miss Owl," said Flying Squirrel.

"Miss Owl has lived in the Night Woods for a long time," said Bat. "She lives in that fine old White Oak Tree near the creek. I'm surprised you don't know her."

"I'm a busy animal, Bat," said Flying Squirrel. "I don't have time to run about here and there talking about nothing to nobody."

"I certainly wouldn't call Miss Owl a 'nobody,'" said Bat.

"Well, *I* think she's a nobody," said Flying Squirrel. "In fact, I don't think there is such a creature."

"What do you mean?" said Bat.

"When I see a skunk I do not see an owl," said Flying Squirrel. "I see a skunk."

"I think we should fly over and look again," said Bat. "Maybe you are right. I've never been famous for my eyesight."

"I'm going to do just that," said Flying Squirrel. "I like to see things for myself. That's why I'm a success." Flying Squirrel got set to jump. Then he leaped into space, spreading his four legs apart. The air was caught in the fold of loose skin from his front paws to his back paws. He glided smoothly down to the nearest tree. Without stopping, he leaped again. He traveled from treetop to treetop with great speed. "He *almost* flies," thought Bat as he watched. "Surely no other animal comes closer to flying."

When Flying Squirrel came to the creek, he glided to the ground.

"My gosh!" he said. His eyes were larger than ever. "Look at that!"

Miss Owl was perched on the lowest branch of a large oak tree. She was beautiful.

Bat landed on the branch next to Miss Owl. "Good evening, Miss Owl," he said. "I'd like you to meet a friend of mine.

Flying Squirrel, this is Miss Owl."

"I'm happy to meet you," said Miss Owl. Flying Squirrel couldn't say a word.

"Flying Squirrel thought you were Chief Skunk," said Bat.

"Oh my goodness," said Miss Owl. "Whatever gave you that idea, Mr. Squirrel?"

"Uh . . . well . . . uh . . . ," said Flying Squirrel.

"Do I look like Chief Skunk?" said Miss Owl.

"NO!" shouted Flying Squirrel. He walked slowly toward Miss Owl. "Not a bit." He climbed the tree and came out on the branch where Miss Owl and Bat were sitting. He sat down next to Miss Owl and looked up at her. She was much larger than he was.

"Miss Owl," he said quietly, "you are the most beautiful lady I have ever seen. Will you marry me?"

Miss Owl threw her head back and

laughed. "Oh Mr. Bat," she said, "your friend has such a wonderful sense of humor." She turned to Flying Squirrel. "Of course I'll marry you, kind sir," she said. "When shall we get married?" She laughed again.

"Thank you! Thank you! How about tomorrow?" said Flying Squirrel. "You've made me the happiest animal in the Night Woods."

Miss Owl was still laughing. "Where have you been hiding him?" she said to Bat. "He's wonderful! If I didn't know better, I'd almost think he wasn't joking."

"Joking?" said Flying Squirrel. "Who's joking?"

"I don't think he is joking," said Bat.

"Of course I'm not joking," said Flying Squirrel. "I *mean* it, Miss Owl. I want you to marry me."

Chief Skunk

A FEW days later Bat answered a knock at his door. It was Police Chief Skunk.

"May I come in, Bat?" he asked.

"Of course, Chief," said Bat. "Come in." He pointed to a chair. "Sit down. I'm always glad to see you. How have you been?"

Chief Skunk walked slowly into the room. Bat had never seen him in a hurry. "I'm fine," he said, looking around for a comfortable chair. "But I have bad news." He sat down. "Miss Owl has disappeared. I've been making a tree-to-tree hunt. I'm trying to find someone who might know something about it."

"What do you mean, 'disappeared?'" said Bat.

"She's vanished! Gone without a clue," said Chief Skunk. He filled his corncob pipe and lit it. "Have you seen her lately, by any chance?"

"Yes I have," said Bat. "And I'm beginning to get a terrible idea."

"What do you mean?" said Chief Skunk. He leaned forward, puffing his pipe.

"I hate to say this," said Bat, "because he's a very good friend of mine. But — did you check with Flying Squirrel?"

Bat told the Chief of Flying Squirrel's meeting with Miss Owl. "He had made up his mind to marry her. But she just laughed at him. I'm afraid F.S. can't take 'no' for an answer."

"Ah-ha!" said Chief Skunk. "That may be why he acted so strange when I saw him."

"What did he do?" said Bat.

"It's what he *didn't* do that was so strange," said Chief Skunk. "He's always polite to me. And he usually asks me to come in and see his latest invention. He thinks he's a mechanical genius, you know."

"Yes, I know," said Bat. "What happened?"

"Well, he wasn't polite," said Chief Skunk. "In fact, he was rude. He didn't ask me into his apartment either."

"Did he answer your questions?"

"He said he knew Miss Owl," said the Chief. "But he didn't know where she was."

"Was he worried about her?" Bat asked.

"Not a bit."

"Doesn't that seem odd to you?" said Bat. "The other day he was in love with her. Now you tell him Miss Owl has disappeared and he wasn't at all worried."

"I'll bet he knows where she is," said Chief Skunk. "I wonder why he won't tell us."

"I'm afraid," said Bat. "I'm afraid he has kidnapped her and is holding her captive somewhere."

"Good heavens!" said Chief Skunk. "If what you say is true, it's the worst crime that has happened in the Night Woods since I became the Police Chief."

"What are we going to do?" said Bat.

"We're going to Flying Squirrel's apartment right now," said Chief Skunk. "If what you say is true, I'll arrest F.S. and hold him for trial at the Night Court."

"And if he's found guilty?" Bat asked.

"If he's found guilty he'll be in trouble, believe me. Judge Bullfrog will send him to Far Island and throw away the key."

The Night Court

"ORDER in the court! Order in the court!" It was Judge Bullfrog's deep voice. "Chief Skunk! You will have to keep Mr. Flying Squirrel quiet. We can't hear Miss Owl."

"Yes sir, Your Honor," said Chief Skunk. He was holding Flying Squirrel down in his seat with one paw. He held the other paw over the squirrel's mouth to keep him from talking. "Now listen, F.S.!" he whispered. "Are you going to be quiet?"

Flying Squirrel nodded.

Chief Skunk let go. "You better do what the judge says. You're already in trouble."

The Night Court met every Tuesday after the full moon. The usual meeting place was near the tree stump at Pollywog Pond. Almost all the night animals came to watch. Judge Bullfrog sat upon the stump and listened to all the cases. A jury was chosen from among the animals of the Night Woods. They had to decide whether the animal on trial was guilty or not guilty.

Tonight Flying Squirrel was on trial for kidnapping Miss Owl. The jury had to decide if he had kept her a prisoner against her will.

Old Judge Bullfrog looked down from the tree stump. "Now then, Miss Owl," he said, "you were telling the court how Flying Squirrel treated you."

"He was very kind to me, Judge,"

said Miss Owl. "He said I could have anything I wanted except my freedom."

"Will you tell the jury why Flying Squirrel was holding you prisoner?"

The night animals began whispering to each other. "Quiet!" called the judge.

Miss Owl turned to face the twelve animals on the jury. They all looked at her.

"He wanted to marry me, that's why!" said Miss Owl. "He said he was going to keep me prisoner until I promised to marry him."

A few of the animals on the jury laughed. Some of the other animals laughed too.

"I don't see anything funny in what happened to me," said Miss Owl to the judge.

"I don't either," said Judge Bullfrog in his deep voice. "Now, members of the jury, is Flying Squirrel guilty or not guilty? I want you to think carefully before you decide anything. You have a great responsibility."

The jury foreman, a toad, stood up. "I think we've already decided," he said. He looked at the other animals. They nodded.

"Flying Squirrel, will you please stand up and face the jury," said Judge Bullfrog.

Flying Squirrel didn't move. Chief Skunk poked him. "Get up, Flying Squirrel, and face the jury," he whispered.

Slowly the little animal stood up.

"What do you say, Mr. Toad?" said Judge Bullfrog. "Is he guilty or not guilty?"

Everything was quiet. The audience leaned forward to hear.

"Guilty, Your Honor," said the toad in a loud, clear voice.

Flying Squirrel slumped to the ground. Chief Skunk tried to get him to his feet.

Bat left his seat in the courtroom and ran to help.

"Get away from me, Bat!" screamed Flying Squirrel. "I don't need any help from you. You're a traitor! You're the one that told them where she was."

Bat moved away. He looked upset. "I'm sorry, F.S.," he said. "I had to."

"I hate you!" yelled Flying Squirrel.

"Order in the court!" shouted Judge Bullfrog. He pounded on the tree stump with his powerful leg. "Order in the court! Chief Skunk — keep that animal quiet even if you have to sit on him."

"Yes sir," said Chief Skunk.

The judge thanked the jury. "I believe you did the right thing," he said. "As for you, Flying Squirrel — it's my duty to sentence you. But first, I want to say a few words about your crime. In the name of 'love,' you tried to take away Miss Owl's freedom. What kind of love is that? If you really loved Miss Owl you would want her to be happy. You're a selfish animal, Flying Squirrel. And because of your selfishness you have committed a crime."

Judge Bullfrog leaned forward on the stump. "Do you have anything to say before I sentence you?"

"Yes I do!" Flying Squirrel pulled himself away from Chief Skunk. "I haven't done anything wrong. I've *always* worked hard to get what I wanted. You're all jealous of me because I'm a success. If you think I'm going to stay in jail, you're crazy! You'll never keep me there. I'll escape!" He turned and pointed at Bat. "And when I do, the first animal I'm going to get even with is that traitor, Bat! You'll be sorry, Bat!" he screamed.

Judge Bullfrog thumped his foot on the tree stump. "Order in the court!" he roared. "Flying Squirrel — I sentence you to jail on Far Island for two years. Chief Skunk, take him away!"

Prison

BAD CREEK ran through the Night Woods toward the south. Far Island was in the middle of it. The worst criminals were kept there as punishment for their crimes. The island was in the widest part of the creek. Rushing water and dangerous rapids flowed past it. The trip to Far Island was by ferry boat. Only Chief Skunk knew how to get to the island safely.

"There's just one other prisoner on the island at this time," said Chief Skunk. He was steering the flat-bottomed boat toward the island.

"What do I care?" said Flying Squirrel. "I'm not going to talk to any criminals."

"Well, you'd better care about this one — it's Weasel. My advice is to stay away from him," said the chief. The glow from his pipe lighted up his face. "He's no good and never will be."

"I talk to anyone I want to talk to," said the squirrel. "And I don't need your advice."

"Suit yourself," said Chief Skunk. "I've warned you."

The ferry boat passed the last few dangerous rocks. At last they were standing on a shaky wooden dock. Chief Skunk began to take some large boxes off the boat. These were the food supplies for the prisoners.

Flying Squirrel looked around. The

island was small. There were no trees. Tall grass and bushes grew right down to the water's edge.

Flying Squirrel felt uneasy. Then he knew why: The night sounds were missing. There were no animals on the island to make the usual noises. The only thing he could hear was the water. It gurgled and hissed loudly as it tumbled downstream.

"I'm not going to stay here," Flying Squirrel said to himself. "This is a crazy place."

Chief Skunk piled the last box of supplies on the dock. "All right. That's done. It'll be enough for the two of you until I come again to get Weasel. He's due to leave here in a few weeks."

Flying Squirrel sat down on one of the boxes. Chief Skunk steered his boat into the creek. The squirrel watched him until he was out of sight. Even when he couldn't see the boat, he could tell where it was by the dim light from Chief Skunk's pipe.

Flying Squirrel sat still for a long time. He wondered how he would ever escape from Far Island. If only there were one tall tree on the island. With a good wind blowing behind him, he might be able to glide across the water.

"I'll find a way to escape," thought Flying Squirrel. "When I make up my mind to do something, I *do* it!"

"That's why I'm a success," he said aloud.

Suddenly an animal with a long neck and little head leaped from the bushes onto the dock. "Success!" he shouted. "Did I hear the word 'success'? Welcome to Far Island, the home of the most successful animals."

"You must be Weasel," said Flying Squirrel.

"I am Weasel, at your service," said the animal. He began to tear the supply boxes apart. "What did the old skunk leave us this time?" He grabbed a can and looked at it closely. "Tomato soup!" he yelled. Then he threw the can as far as he could into the creek.

"Hey! What are you doing?" said Flying Squirrel. "That's our food."

"Please," said Weasel. He held up his paw to silence Flying Squirrel. "Don't use that wonderful word 'food' when you talk about this slop."

"What do you mean?" said the squirrel.

"I'm talking about this soup," said Weasel. "I'm starting to feel like a wet sponge from eating nothing but soup."

"That's all there is?"

"That's all there ever is," said Weasel. "That — and a little honey now and then."

"Honey?"

"Yeah. The only other living thing on

this island, besides us, is a bunch of bees."

Flying Squirrel began to tear the boxes apart. Sure enough, every one of them was filled with cans of soup.

"See! See!" screamed Weasel. He did a dance around the pile of cans. "Barley soup, bean soup, tomato soup too. I hate soup, and so will you." Each time he circled the stack of cans he threw one of them into the creek.

"Stop it!" yelled Flying Squirrel. He grabbed Weasel and tried to stop him. "Whatever it is, it's all we have to eat until Chief Skunk comes back."

Escape from Far Island

FLYING SQUIRREL used the first few nights on Far Island to look over the place. From one end to the other it was exactly the same: bushes and grass, grass and bushes.

In the center of the island was a large rock. Flying Squirrel often stood on the rock and looked across the creek at the Night Woods. On a bright night he could sometimes see one of the animals. Then he would yell at the top of his voice. No one ever heard him. He guessed that the noise of the roaring water drowned him out.

Every night Flying Squirrel talked to Weasel. He told him over and over what had happened. "That Bat!" he said. "And I thought he was my friend."

One night Weasel said, "You really hate Bat, don't you? But how about Miss Owl? Do you still want to marry her?"

"Who?" said Flying Squirrel.

"Miss Owl," said Weasel. "Don't tell me you've forgotten her?"

"I guess I had," said Flying Squirrel. "I've been so mad, she went right out of my mind." He pounded one paw into the other. "I'll do anything to get even with Bat," he said. "And I mean *anything.*"

"Suppose I fixed it up for you to get off this island so you could get even with Bat," said Weasel. "What would you do for me?"

"What do you want?"

"How about half of everything you own?"

"Half! You're crazy! I own an apartment tree and lots of mechanical inventions. I'm one of the richest animals in the woods."

"Make me your partner, then. We can share everything you own," said Weasel. "With my brains and your money we could make a good team."

"I wouldn't share anything with you," said Flying Squirrel. "Besides — how do I know you can be trusted? You're a crook. You *can't* be trusted."

"It's up to you," said Weasel. He walked away.

Soon the time came for Weasel to leave the island. His sentence of three years was finished. Chief Skunk was coming any night, so Weasel waited at the dock. He had written a paper making himself Flying Squirrel's partner. He held it in front of the little squirrel's nose.

"Sign it! Sign it!" he yelled. "Sign it before it's too late. I'll leave and you'll lose your last chance. You're going to be on this island for two years. *Two long years!*"

Flying Squirrel thought about Bat flying around the Night Woods enjoying himself. And here he was — stuck on this island for two years. If only he were free — just long enough to get revenge on Bat. The thought kept going around in his head over and over again.

Suddenly Weasel shouted, "Here comes Skunk! See — there's the light from his pipe."

Flying Squirrel grabbed the paper away from Weasel. "I'll sign it! I'll sign it!" he said. "But first you have to tell me your plan. How can I get off this island?"

"Come," said Weasel. "There's time. Follow me!" He darted into the bushes. They ran to the large rock in the center of the island. "Here — help me give it a push," said Weasel.

The two animals pushed and tugged at the rock. There was a hole under it.

"There," said Weasel. "I've been digging this tunnel for three years. It will take you right under Bad Creek to the Night Woods."

"Wait a minute," said Flying Squirrel. "I'm not dumb. You can't fool me. If this tunnel goes to the Night Woods, why haven't you taken it yourself?"

"The answer to that question is sad."

"What do you mean?"

"By the time I dug all the way to the Night Woods my sentence was almost up," said Weasel. "So I said to myself, what's the use of escaping now? Chief Skunk is going to set me free anyhow.

If I had escaped, I would have been a hunted animal, see?"

"That makes sense," said Flying Squirrel. He jumped into the hole. "So long — thanks for everything."

"Hey!" shouted Weasel. "Wait! You didn't sign the paper."

Flying Squirrel placed the paper against the smooth rock and signed it. "It's worth it," he said. "Anything is worth it to get off this island and get even with Bat."

"Now you're being smart," said Weasel. "Good-bye and good luck."

Flying Squirrel went quickly into the tunnel.

He felt his way slowly along the wall. The tunnel went downhill at first. Then it was level. "I must be under the creek," thought Flying Squirrel. "It's damp here."

After a while the tunnel began to rise.

Suddenly the little squirrel saw a glimmer of light ahead.

"That must be the moonlight shining through the end of the tunnel," he said. He kept his eyes on the dim light and hurried on. Faster and faster he went. "I'm free! I'm free!" he shouted. He was running now. When he came to the opening, he gave a mighty leap. He rushed from the tunnel and fell headlong into the dark waters of Bad Creek.

"I've been tricked!" he screamed. The water pounded down on top of him. The sharp black rocks were everywhere. He fought to stay on top of the water. The tumbling, churning water swept him downstream. And then he went under.

Mother Squirrel's
Syrup Factory

FLYING SQUIRREL sank toward the bottom of Bad Creek. He thought his life was over. Then he remembered something Bat had said: "A drowning animal sinks three times before he dies."

The little squirrel kicked and paddled hard with his paws. "I'm going to get my three chances," he decided, "just like everybody else."

He swam back up to the surface. The water pounded him again and he went under. "Once more," he said. He used all the strength he had and fought back to the surface. There — right in front of him — was a log. He grabbed it and held on as hard as he could.

The log wasn't a very good boat. It crashed into rocks. It spun around in the water until Flying Squirrel was dizzy.

It was under the water as often as it was on top of it. Flying Squirrel never let go. This was his last chance and he knew it.

At last the log came out of the rapids. The sharp rocks were left behind. Now the log moved smoothly along the gentle waters of Bad Creek.

Flying Squirrel lay on the log. He was alive, but he was very weak — too weak to swim ashore.

Hours later the log came to rest on the bank of the creek. Flying Squirrel dragged himself onto the shore and fell asleep at once.

He slept through the daylight hours of the next day. And the night was halfway gone before he awoke. For a long time he lay face down. He thought about all that had happened to him. Things couldn't have been much worse. Everything was gone: He had lost his money, his reputation, and his freedom.

But he was alive! Yes, he was alive. He had lived through everything. At last he rolled over and sat up.

It was a beautiful night. The moon was shining softly through the willow trees. Here and there pinpoint lights of fireflies flashed in the darkness. Flying Squirrel listened. A hum of crickets filled his ear. He heard the peep-peep-peep of a nearby frog.

"This place reminds me of something," he thought. "I wonder what."

Flying Squirrel looked around for the tallest tree. He saw a feathery white pine. It stood on high ground, taller than the rest of the trees. He climbed to the top of it and looked in every direction.

"I've been here before," he thought. "But I can't remember where it is."

Suddenly he had a strange feeling. What was it? He took a deep breath, thinking hard . . . and then, he remembered!

The little squirrel leaped into space. With all four legs spread apart, the air was caught in the fold of loose skin. He glided swiftly down for a hundred feet or more. Thump, he landed and tumbled on the grass.

Flying Squirrel dashed across a clearing and into the underbrush. He stopped. Straight ahead was the first tree in the world. He climbed the great trunk. In a moment he was among the branches in front of the door of his childhood home.

On the door was an old sign. It was hard to read because half the letters were worn away. But Flying Squirrel knew what the sign said — he had read it every day when he was a boy: "Mother Squirrel's Maple Syrup Factory. Open six nights a week. Closed Sunday."

Flying Squirrel knocked on the door.

After a short wait he heard his mother's voice. "We're not open tonight. Can't you read the sign? It's Sunday — come back tomorrow night."

"Hey Ma! I don't want any maple syrup," said Flying Squirrel. "It's me — your son."

"Dee-Dee!" said Mother Squirrel. She opened the door. "I don't believe it. You've come home."

"I can hardly believe it myself, Ma," said Flying Squirrel.

"Come in, come in," said Mother Squirrel. "Let me look at you, my baby."

"Ma, I'm not your baby any more," said Flying Squirrel.

"You'll always be my baby," said

Mother Squirrel. She pulled him into the room. "Now sit down. I want to look at you."

Flying Squirrel sat in a chair next to the fireplace.

"Why you look fine, son. Just fine," said Mother Squirrel. "Oh my, you must be a big success. I always knew you would be." She took out a handkerchief and wiped her eyes. "I wish you would stay here and help me run the business."

Flying Squirrel looked around the room. Everything was the same as when he was young. Even the pictures hung crookedly on the walls as he remembered.

"How *is* the business, Ma? How's it going?"

"Not so good, son," said Mother Squirrel. "The machinery is old. It's breaking down all the time now. I can't repair it and I can't find anyone who can do a good job. I'm losing all my old customers. I can't fill their orders for syrup fast enough."

Flying Squirrel jumped from his seat. "Ma! Don't you remember? I'm the greatest fixer of machinery there is." He took off his ragged scarf. "Let's go! Show me something that's broken."

"Now? Before you've had anything to eat?"

"Now!" said Flying Squirrel. "I never felt more like fixing things than I do right now."

The Dark Cloud

ONE week later Judge Bullfrog had a
meeting with Bat and Chief Skunk. They
sat around a table in the Judge's office
under the tree stump at Pollywog Pond.

"I can't find anything wrong with
Weasel's paper," said Judge Bullfrog.
"I've looked at it carefully. It's Flying
Squirrel's signature all right."

"But, Judge," said Bat. "Why would
Flying Squirrel want to become partners
with a crook like Weasel?"

"I don't know," said the judge. "And if he was killed trying to escape from Far Island we may never know."

"If you ask me," said Chief Skunk, "Weasel tricked him into signing the paper. Then he got rid of him somehow."

"That's only a guess," said Judge Bullfrog. "You've got to have proof, you know that. In the meantime, I've decided that everything Flying Squirrel owns belongs to Weasel."

"Come on, Chief," said Bat. "We're wasting our time here."

"Sorry, boys," said Judge Bullfrog, "but that's the law."

Later that night Bat flew home. As he came near the Sycamore Arms, he saw Flying Squirrel's window being opened. Quickly, he flew into the shadows of the tree next door. He saw that it was only Weasel, the new owner, opening the window. Weasel had moved right in to Flying Squirrel's apartment.

"I'm getting jumpy over nothing," Bat said to himself.

Just as Bat came out of the shadows, Weasel stuck his head out of the window and whistled. Bat hid himself again. A dark cloud came out of the window and disappeared into the darkness. Weasel closed the window.

Bat was puzzled. What was the dark cloud? Where did it go? Was Weasel up to something? Bat decided to wait and watch the window.

About thirty minutes later the window opened again. Weasel stuck his head out and looked around. This time he whistled twice. A dark cloud came sailing down out of the sky. Only this time it was different. It was fluttering wildly.

Was it the same cloud? Bat wasn't sure. It floated through the window. Weasel closed the window and Bat couldn't see any more.

Bat went to police headquarters and told Chief Skunk what he had seen. The chief sat in front of a roll-top desk and puffed his pipe. "That's strange," he said. "I wonder what it means?"

"He's up to something," said Bat.

"What?"

"Can't you break in there and find out?"

"Hold on there, Bat," said Chief Skunk. "I've been thinking over our talk with the judge. He's right, you know."

"You mean we've got to have proof?"

"That's exactly what I mean," said Chief Skunk.

"I suppose you're right," said Bat.

"There's no proof of wrong-doing in what you've told me," said the chief.

"What can we do?" said Bat.

"Watch him!" said Chief Skunk. "I'm going around there first thing tomorrow night. We'll watch him twenty-four hours a day."

Bat flew home. He poured himself a glass of milk. Then he sat in the leather chair in his den. He thought and thought. All he could think of were questions. There were no answers.

He was sitting in his best thinking position, feet up and eyes closed, when his wife came in.

"Oh, there you are, Bat," she said. "Help me zip up this dress, will you?"

While Bat helped his wife, he told her what he'd been thinking about.

"Bat, you're making a mountain out of a molehill," said Mrs. Bat. "I want you to promise to stay away from Weasel."

"You know something?" said Bat. "I know Weasel has been a criminal. Maybe that's why I keep thinking he's up to something crooked."

"You think too much, Bat. That's your trouble."

"Perhaps if someone treated Weasel

kindly for a change, he'd be a better animal," said Bat.

"Now, Bat — don't you go getting ideas," said Mrs. Bat.

"That settles it," said Bat. "I'm sure of it. I'm going up there and ask him a few questions — in a friendly way."

"Don't you dare bring him down here," said Mrs. Bat.

Bat flew up the tree to Weasel's apartment. He knocked on the door. He waited a few moments and knocked again. Suddenly the dark cloud came out of an upstairs window and sailed down upon him.

Raccoon and Badger

"WHY do you have to leave, Dee-Dee? You've only been here a week," said Mother Squirrel.

Flying Squirrel and his mother were looking out of the window of the syrup factory.

"Look at the line of customers," said Mother Squirrel. "And we're not even open yet."

"Just like in the old days, hey, Ma?" said Flying Squirrel.

"Better, son. There are a lot of new customers out there."

"I should stay," said Flying Squirrel. "I like it here. And there's work for me . . . but . . ."

"No 'buts' about it," said Mother Squirrel. "Unpack that bag."

"I can't, Ma. Really."

"Why not, son? This is your home."

"I've got to go, Ma. There is something I have to take care of."

"Will you ever come back?"

"Gosh, I hope so, Ma."

"You're in trouble, aren't you?"

"It's nothing for you to worry about, Ma."

"Well, you know what you have to do, son. God bless you. You've made your old mother happy with your visit," said Mother Squirrel. She hugged him. "Be sure and take the lunch I packed for you."

"It's in the suitcase, Ma. So long."

"Good-bye, Dee-Dee."

Flying Squirrel knew that Chief Skunk

would put him in jail on sight. But he had thought of a way to fool Chief Skunk and all the other animals who knew him. He walked a short way until he was out of sight. Then he hid behind a tree and put on some of his mother's old clothes. He sprinkled some flour in his hair to make it look gray.

He also brought along an old ear trumpet he had found in the attic. It had belonged to his grandmother who was hard of hearing. She had used it to hear better. Flying Squirrel thought it would help make him look like a very old lady.

He put the ear trumpet to his ear and he started walking again. He walked slowly, like an old lady. Soon he came upon a raccoon by the side of the road. The raccoon was having trouble starting his car.

Flying Squirrel stopped and introduced himself. He tried to talk like an

old lady. "I wonder if you are going in my direction," he said. "And would you give me a ride?"

"Lady," said the raccoon. "I can't give nobody a ride because I can't get this so-called car started."

"What did you say?" said Flying Squirrel. He wiggled the ear trumpet, pretending he couldn't hear.

The raccoon yelled into the ear trumpet: "I can't start this car!"

Flying Squirrel almost jumped, the voice was so loud. "Oh dear," he said. He tried to keep his voice high. "What seems to be the trouble?"

"Now don't that beat all," said Raccoon. He shouted again, "Are you a mechanic, lady?" Then he laughed and slapped his knee.

"As a matter of fact," said Flying Squirrel, "I may be able to help you. My son is a master mechanic and a great inventor. He has taught me a good deal."

After much talking back and forth, Flying Squirrel was allowed to look at the engine. "Why, this is simple," he said. "Your carburetor is flooding. You really need a new one. I'll fix it for now. It'll be good enough to get us to the nearest garage."

Flying Squirrel hitched up his skirts and bent over the engine. Soon he had it running nicely.

"Hey, lady! You really *are* a mechanic," said Raccoon. "Hop in the back of the car. I'll take you to the nearest town."

The little squirrel climbed into the dark back seat. The car started moving. Flying Squirrel saw there was someone on the seat with him. "Oh, how do you do?" he said in his old lady's voice. "I didn't see you."

The car speeded down the road. Raccoon grinned over his shoulder. "Don't expect an answer from him. He don't talk much."

"What did you say?" said Flying

Squirrel. He turned the ear trumpet toward Raccoon.

"He don't talk much!" shouted Raccoon.

Raccoon lowered his voice. "Now listen, Badge," he said. "The old lady is deaf. Just keep your voice down and we can talk."

A grunt came from the corner.

"We're lucky. We can use her. We ain't got time to go to no garage," said Raccoon. "She can keep the car going if it stops again, see?"

Another grunt.

"Test the batteries in the flashlight. We don't want anything to go wrong."

A light flashed on. Flying Squirrel looked quickly into the corner. The quiet animal was a mean-looking badger. The little squirrel looked out the window. What had he gotten himself into? Who were these animals? Where were they going?

The Bank Robbery

RACCOON stepped on the gas. The car went faster and faster.

"It's just like the old days," said Raccoon. "Only this time nobody's going to get caught. Weasel's too smart for them. Last night Weasel's cousin and Possum robbed a bank miles away from here. Tonight it's our turn. Then, tomorrow night it will be their turn again." He laughed. "Everybody will be running around in circles trying to figure it out."

The badger didn't answer. He moved forward in his seat. Flying Squirrel shivered. He could see that this badger was a powerful animal. These guys must be up to something crooked. Who was the 'Weasel' they were talking about? Was it the same Weasel who had almost killed him?

Raccoon spoke again. "With that Sycamore Arms Apartment Tree in the Night Woods, we got the perfect setup."

Flying Squirrel's heart beat faster. So it *was* the same Weasel.

Raccoon looked at his watch. "We're right on time. All we have to do is make sure the money is ready when they come. He has them trained to come *exactly* on time."

Suddenly the car stopped.

"Here we are," said Raccoon. "And there's the bank." He kept the engine running. "Listen, Grandma!" he shouted into the ear trumpet. "Wait in the car a few minutes. We'll be right back." He grinned. "We have to make a withdrawal from the bank."

"I'll get in the front seat and keep the engine running," said Flying Squirrel.

Badger followed Raccoon into an alley near the bank.

Flying Squirrel waited for the two animals to get out of sight. Then he drove the car around the corner to a phone booth. He called the police station and told them that Raccoon and Badger were robbing the bank.

"Who is this?" said the policeman.

"A friend," said Flying Squirrel. He hung up. Then he ran to a store near the bank and waited in the shadows. Suddenly a dark cloud appeared in the night sky above the bank. It sailed through an open window.

Then Flying Squirrel heard the sirens wailing. Three police cars with flashing red lights came down the street. Just

before they got to the bank, Flying Squirrel saw another dark cloud. Or was it the same cloud? This time it was flying away from the bank. It seemed to flutter as it went.

The police cars surrounded the bank. The policemen got out and ducked down behind the cars. The largest policeman spoke through a megaphone. "All right, Raccoon and Badger! We know you're there. Come out with your hands up!"

"Don't shoot!" shouted Raccoon from within the bank. "We're coming out."

The door of the bank opened. The two animals came out with their hands over their heads.

"Well, well. What do you think you're up to?" said the large policeman.

"Nothing," said Raccoon. "We weren't doing nothing."

"Search them!" said the policeman. "Get the money."

One of the other policemen searched

Raccoon and Badger. "They don't have any money," he said.

"It must be in the bank or the alley. They haven't had time to hide it," said the large policeman. "Find it!" Some of the policemen ran to carry out his order.

"You won't find no money," said Raccoon. "There wasn't none in the bank. Was there, Badge?"

"That's not funny," said the policeman. "There was lots of money in that bank."

"You can't arrest us for stealing," said Raccoon. "We didn't take any money out of the bank."

"I can arrest you for breaking into the bank," said the policeman. "You must know where the money is."

"It's not fair!" shouted Raccoon.

"Tell it to the judge," said the policeman. "Lock them up, boys."

Flying Squirrel could hardly believe what he had seen. What did it mean? Where was the money? He was sure

Raccoon knew where it was. All of this had something to do with Weasel. But what?

And what was the mysterious dark cloud? He wanted to tell the policemen about it but he was afraid to. He was afraid they would discover he was an escaped prisoner — afraid they would think he was part of the gang. Flying Squirrel didn't know what to do.

The Mystery Solved

"DO hold still, Bat," said Mrs. Bat. "I'm
almost finished." Mrs. Bat was putting a
handkerchief around her husband's head.

"Oh! Oh, my head!" said Bat.

"What on earth happened to you?"
said Mrs. Bat. "Your head is swollen like
a balloon. And it's all bumpy."

"I don't know," said Bat. "The last
thing I remember, I was knocking on
Weasel's door. Then I heard that terrible
buzzing in my. ears."

"What was it?"

"I don't know," said Bat. "After that I must have fallen and hit my head."

"From way up there? It's a wonder you weren't killed."

There was a sharp knock at the door.

"That must be Chief Skunk," said Mrs. Bat. "I sent for him as soon as I found you."

"Be careful," said Bat. "Make sure it's the chief. There's something strange going on around here."

Mrs. Bat peeked through the window. "It's Chief Skunk all right. If I didn't see him, I could still smell the pipe smoke."

Chief Skunk came into the room faster than usual. "Bat, you look awful."

"Isn't it terrible?" said Mrs. Bat.

"What happened?" asked Chief Skunk.

Bat told his story to the chief. "And that's all I know," he said. "What do you think it means?"

"It's hard to tell," said the chief. "That buzzing noise you heard — was it inside your head or did you really hear it?"

"I think I heard it," said Bat. "It happened so fast, I'm not sure."

"You *heard* it, Bat," said a voice from the window. "It didn't happen in your head."

"Good heavens!" said Chief Skunk. "That voice. It's . . ."

"FLYING SQUIRREL!" shouted Bat. He ran to the window. "It's you, old friend! You're alive!"

Bat opened the door and pulled Flying Squirrel into the room. "Look! He's alive! You're alive!"

"Bat — you shouldn't be on your feet," said Mrs. Bat. She tried to push Bat into a chair. "You've just had a terrible blow on your head."

Bat paid no attention to her. "What happened to you?" he said to Flying Squirrel. "Where have you been? Why are you dressed like an old lady?" Bat kept shaking Flying Squirrel's paw as he talked. "It's amazing! We thought you were dead."

"I wanted to get revenge on you, Bat," said Flying Squirrel. "But that's all forgotten now."

"You'll have to go back to Far Island," said Chief Skunk.

"I'm ready," said Flying Squirrel. "I've been following you around trying to get up courage to turn myself in. But first, I'm going to help you catch the head of the Weasel Gang, Weasel himself."

"What do you know about Weasel?" said Chief Skunk. "What *gang* are you talking about? When you spoke from the window just now, you said Bat heard the buzzing noise. How did you know?"

"Yes, F.S." said Bat. "What do you know about this mystery?"

"I was just as mixed up as you two are," said Flying Squirrel, "until I heard

Bat's story as I was waiting outside the window. Now I think I know what's been going on. And what's more, I have a plan to catch Weasel red-handed."

"What *has* been going on?" said Chief Skunk. "Perhaps you had better tell us everything you know."

Flying Squirrel sat down in Bat's favorite chair. Bat brought him some milk and cookies. He sipped the milk and ate the cookies as he told the story.

He told how Weasel had tricked him into signing the paper. He told how he had almost lost his life in Bad Creek. He told about his mother and the syrup factory.

Then he told of his meeting with Raccoon and Badger. He told what they said when they thought he couldn't hear them.

At last he told of the bank robbery — and about the mysterious cloud.

"Why, that's exactly what I saw," said

Bat. "The same kind of dark cloud."

"When I heard your story that the dark cloud came from Weasel's apartment," said Flying Squirrel, "I remembered something Weasel told me when we were on Far Island together."

"What?" said Chief Skunk.

"He said the only other living thing on the island was a bunch of bees," said Flying Squirrel.

"What does that have to do with it?" said Bat.

"Don't you see?" said Flying Squirrel. "Don't you see what's happening?"

Chief Skunk shook his head slowly. "Frankly, I don't."

"Tell us! Tell us!" said Bat. "Stop teasing."

"The mysterious dark cloud is made up of thousands of bees," said Flying Squirrel.

"Bees!" said Chief Skunk. His pipe fell in his lap.

"That's the buzzing you heard, Bat. Your swollen head is caused by bee bites," said Flying Squirrel.

"Good heavens!" said Mrs. Bat.

"Weasel was on Far Island with nothing to do for three years," said Flying Squirrel. "He must have trained the bees."

"But what for?" said Bat. "What are the bees for? What do they do?"

"They bring the money back," said Flying Squirrel. "Weasel's gang work in pairs. They take turns robbing banks. In case they get caught, they never have the money with them. The bees are trained to fly back to Weasel with the money."

"Astounding!" said Bat.

"Each bee carries a bill," said Flying Squirrel.

"That explains the fluttering I saw when the dark cloud returned," said Bat.

"Absolutely amazing!" said Chief

Skunk. "I've never heard of anything so daring in the whole history of crime."

"That's a wonderful bit of detective work," said Bat. "Now, what about your plan? You said you could catch Weasel red-handed. What did you mean?"

"There will probably be another robbery tomorrow night," said Flying Squirrel.

"That's right," said Chief Skunk. "Those other two crooks are still free. Do you know what bank they're going to rob?"

"No," said Flying Squirrel. "But we don't have to. I know of a secret weapon. We can use it to catch Weasel red-handed with the money."

"How?" said Chief Skunk.

"Listen," said Flying Squirrel. "And I'll explain my plan."

Caught Red-handed

THE following night Chief Skunk, Bat, and Flying Squirrel waited near the apartment tree. They stood in the shadows.

"Do you have enough of the stuff?" said Chief Skunk. "It has to be strong enough to work."

"We have two big jars," said Flying Squirrel. "I'll carry one and Bat will carry the other."

"You have to make sure Weasel doesn't see you," said Chief Skunk. "If he does, the plan won't work."

"Don't worry," said Flying Squirrel. "I know that tree like the back of my paw. We'll get up there without any trouble, you'll see."

"I wish I could go up there with you," said the chief. "But I'm not much good at climbing trees."

"We need you down here, anyway," said Bat. "In case he tries to get away, you'll be here to arrest him."

"I guess you're right," said Chief Skunk.

"Shhh," whispered Bat, "somebody's opening the window."

The three animals watched as the window was slowly opened. Weasel stuck his head out and looked around. Then he whistled. The dark cloud of bees came flying out of the open window. They disappeared into the dark sky. Weasel closed the window.

"Now!" said Flying Squirrel. "Now is the time. Let's go!"

"Good luck," whispered Chief Skunk.

Flying Squirrel and Bat ran from the shadows to the bottom of the apartment tree. They went up quietly. When they came to Weasel's apartment, they kept going up. At last they reached the top of the tree. "Are we right over his window?"

"I think so," said Bat. He flew out a little way and looked down. "Yes," he said when he came back, "there it is."

"Well, there's nothing to do now but wait," said Flying Squirrel.

They waited at the top of the tree for the bees to return. It was a warm night. A gentle breeze moved the branches. Flying Squirrel thought of another night at the top of the tree. It was the night he met Miss Owl — the night his troubles began. It seemed so long ago. Had he really been that foolish? "Bat," he whispered, "when I get off Far Island, will you help me set things right with Miss Owl?"

"How's that?" said Bat.

"You know what I need to do," said Flying Squirrel. "Tell me how to apologize to her."

"I don't think you need my help," said Bat. "You seem to be doing everything right these days."

Suddenly they heard the sound of a window being opened.

"That's Weasel!" whispered Flying Squirrel.

"Shall we do it now?"

"No. Wait for the whistle," said Flying Squirrel. "Take the top off your jar and get ready."

The two friends looked down from the top of the tree. Weasel stuck his head out and looked around. Then he whistled twice.

"Now!" said Flying Squirrel.

The animals slowly turned two jars of honey upside-down. The sticky stuff landed on Weasel's head.

"Hey!" shouted Weasel. "What's this?"

The dark cloud of bees came flying down from the sky. Each one was carrying a piece of paper money. They fluttered like green butterflies toward Weasel. He rubbed his eyes and pulled at his ears trying to get the honey off. When the bees smelled the honey they forgot everything Weasel had taught them. A thousand bees landed on Weasel's head, and a thousand pieces of paper money stuck to him.

"I'm getting out of here!" he shouted. He ran down the stairs, out of the tree and into the arms of Chief Skunk.

"You're under arrest, Weasel," said the chief. "That's stolen money."

The End

WEASEL was sent to Far Island for five more years. The members of his gang were captured and sent there with him.

Flying Squirrel was a hero now. Nobody wanted to send him back to Far Island. At Judge Bullfrog's suggestion the Night Court met again and pardoned him. Flying Squirrel was freed because of his help in capturing the Weasel Gang.

And Miss Owl? What happened to her? Did she and Flying Squirrel get married? No, they did not. In a moment of truth, Flying Squirrel realized that, for the time being at least, he would rather remain a bachelor. He and Miss Owl did become best friends, however.